Mudpuddle Farm

SIX ANIMAL ADVENTURES!

michael morpurgo

Cover illustrations by Cecilia Johannson

Interior illustrations by Shoo Rayner

HarperCollins *Children's Books*

For Anna

Mossop's Last Chance first published in hardback by A & C Black (Publishers) Limited 1983
First published in paperback by Collins, a division of HarperCollins *Publishers* Ltd in 1988

Albertine, Goose Queen first published in hardback by A & C Black (Publishers) Limited 1989
First published in paperback by Collins, a division of HarperCollins *Publishers* Ltd in 1990

And Pigs Might Fly first published in hardback by A & C Black (Publishers) Limited 1983
First published in paperback by Collins, a division of HarperCollins *Publishers* Ltd in 1988

Jigger's Day Off first published in hardback by A & C Black (Publishers) Limited 1989
First published in paperback by Collins, a division of HarperCollins *Publishers* Ltd in 1990

Martians at Mudpuddle Farm first published in hardback by A & C Black (Publishers) Limited 1994
First published in paperback by Collins, a division of HarperCollins *Publishers* Ltd in 1995

Mum's the Word first published in hardback by A & C Black (Publishers) Limited 1995
First published in paperback by Collins, a division of HarperCollins *Publishers* Ltd in 1996

This bind-up edition published by HarperCollins *Children's Books* in 2009

HarperCollins *Children's Books* is a division of HarperCollins *Publishers* Ltd,
77-85 Fulham Palace Road, Hammersmith, London W6 8JB.

Visit our website at: www.harpercollins.co.uk

1 3 5 7 9 10 8 6 4 2

ISBN-13: 978-0-00-729666-8

Text copyright © Michael Morpurgo 1983, 1989, 1994, 1995
Cover illustrations copyright © Cecilia Johannson 2008
Interior illustrations copyright © Shoo Rayner, 1983, 1989, 1994, 1995
The author and illustrators assert the moral right to be identified
as the author and illustrators of the work. A CIP catalogue record
for this title is available from the British Library.
All rights reserved.

Printed and bound in England by Clays Ltd, St Ives plc

COCK-A-DOODLE-DOO!

Chapter One

There was once a family of all sorts of animals that lived in the farmyard behind the tumble-down barn on Mudpuddle Farm.

At first light every morning Frederick, the flame-feathered cockerel, lifted his eyes to the sun and crowed and crowed, until the light came on at old Farmer Rafferty's bedroom window.

Mossop was a tired old farm cat who spent most of his day curled up asleep on the seat of Farmer Rafferty's tractor. Mossop paid no attention to Frederick – he got up when he pleased.

GUMLOP XL5

Farmer Rafferty was usually a kind
man with smiling eyes, but like
Mossop he was old and tired, and he
ached in his bones in the wet weather.
His animals were his only friends
and his only family.

You look after me,
and I'll look after you.

Auntie Grace and Primrose let down their milk for him.

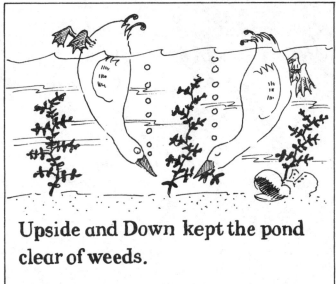

Upside and Down kept the pond clear of weeds.

Captain carried him all around the farm to check the sheep.

Jigger, the almost-always-sensible
sheepdog, rounded up the sheep.

And Mossop was supposed to catch mice and rats.

Chapter Two

Farmer Rafferty always liked to sing as he worked. He sang in a crusty, croaky kind of voice.

la-la-tiddley-um-pom pom-tiddley-um-pom-pom-

That morning though, as old
Farmer Rafferty went into the
tumble-down barn to fetch corn
from the corn bin, he suddenly
stopped singing.

with a hey and a ho and a tiddle-iddle-po-and-a-bing-bang-

Oh!

The animals crowded into the barn
to find out what was the matter.
They found Farmer Rafferty
standing by the corn bin holding a
mouse up by its tail.

This is a mouse, and there are
three more in there, Mossop.

Mossop!   Where is that Mossop?

FARMER'S
WEE...

Have we or have we not got a cat on this farm?' said Farmer Rafferty in the nasty, raspy voice he kept for special occasions.

'We have,' said Auntie Grace, the dreamy-eyed brown cow.

'She's right,' said her friend Primrose, who always agreed with her. 'We have, and he's asleep on the tractor seat.'

'Having a catnap,' sniggered Upside or Down – no one could ever tell which was which.

'Having his beauty sleep,' mumbled Egbert, the greedy, grumbly goat who ate anything and everything. 'Not that it'll help him much.'

'Fetch him,' ordered old Farmer Rafferty. 'Fetch that Mossop here. I have a thing or two to say to him.'

But at that very same moment
Mossop wandered into the barn,
yawning hugely.

MOSSOP!
Everywhere I go these days there's mice or there's rats. There's mice in my barley sacks, there's rats in my roof and now there's mice in my corn bin. I've warned you before and this time I have had enough. If you aren't up to the job, you will have to go. That's all there is to it.
Gulp!

Chapter Three

Mossop knew, and everyone knew,
that Farmer Rafferty always meant
what he said. So the whole day long
Mossop hunted

through the hay barns,

in amongst the barley sacks

and along the rafters.

But it was
no use, his
heart wasn't
in it.

He hadn't caught a mouse for a long time now –

he was too old,

too blind,

too slow,
and he knew it.
Everyone knew it.

That evening, tired and miserable, Mossop made his way back to his sleeping seat on the tractor.

'How many did you catch, Mossop?'
asked Peggoty who lay surrounded
by her piglets on top of the steaming
dung heap.

Peggoty was a practical sort of a
pig. She could add up – which was
more than any of the others could.

'Catch anything, old son?' said
Jigger. Mossop shook his head.
'You've only got to say the word and
I'll give you a hand. Nothing would
give me greater pleasure.'

Captain's right, but thanks anyway Jigger. I'm too old.
Only got one eye and he doesn't work like he should.
And I'm slow as an old carthorse– begging your pardon, Captain. Anyway my claws are scarcely sharp enough to scratch myself.
As for my teeth– I've only got a few of them left and they're not much good anymore.

And all the animals – except one –
gathered round the tractor because
everyone loved Mossop.

But Albertine the goose sat on her
island in the middle of the pond,
and thought deep goosey thoughts.

Everyone agreed with Diana the
silly sheep, which made her very
happy.

'If Mossop can't see well enough,
then he should wear glasses,'
Auntie Grace said. 'That's what
Mr Rafferty does when he's reading.
He sees a lot better that way.'

But somehow that didn't seem to be
a good idea after all.

'If Mossop's claws aren't sharp
enough, we could sharpen them up
on Mr Rafferty's axe grinder,' said
Peggotty. 'Mr Rafferty's axe always
cuts better after it's been sharpened
doesn't it?'

But Mossop didn't think that
sounded much fun either.

Jigger said.
'Mossop could have false teeth like
Farmer Rafferty. After all, old
Farmer Rafferty always eats a lot
better when he's got them in. He
keeps them on the kitchen window
sill. I've seen them.'

So they all went off to look at
Farmer Rafferty's teeth.

But in the end they decided it
wouldn't be fair on Mr Rafferty to
take his false teeth, and anyway
they were far too big for Mossop.

Even Egbert the goat
tried to think, but he
found that a bit
difficult, so he ate a
paper sack instead.

Everyone thought . . . except Mossop,
who was far too tired to do
anything but sleep.

Chapter Four

Out on the island in the middle of her pond Albertine sat all by herself and thought deep, secret, goosey thoughts.

She rose to her feet, flapped her
great white wings and honked until
everyone gathered at the water's
edge in high excitement.

When Captain had calmed them
down, she spoke, and everyone
listened. They knew that Albertine
was a very clever goose.

Go to every mouse hole and every rat hole. Tell them all that they must come to the barn for a meeting.
But what if they won't come?
Just tell them that if they don't come there will soon be a new sharp-eyed, sharp-clawed cat on the farm. They'll come alright. You'll see.
What's it all about?
I don't know.
Good old Albertine.

Within minutes every mouse and every rat on the farm had gathered in the tumble-down barn.

Captain called the meeting to order, but the mice and rats all threatened to leave because Jigger was licking his lips.

Captain told Peggoty to sit on the dog's tail, just in case.

Albertine rose to speak.

Mice, rats and rodents all,
welcome.

And she told them her master plan.
They listened hard – except for one
little mouse who was playing chase
in the corner with Pintsize,
the tiniest piglet.

'How many of you are there?' asked Albertine politely, when she had finished.
'A hundred and twenty-five, Guv'nor, including the little'uns,'
said the spokesrat, after proper consultations with the spokesmouse.

But Peggoty the practical pig knew better.

A hundred and twenty-six to be precise.

If you say so, Porker.

'Never mind. That will be quite enough for what I have in mind,' said Albertine, smiling.

Chapter Five

Mossop woke from his comfortable
dreams on the tractor seat and saw
the sun sinking through the trees.
He knew the time had come for him
to leave. Sadly he said goodbye to
all his old friends.

Everyone was there to see him off
except for Upside and Down who
never missed their tea, not for
anything.

There were tears in Mossop's eyes as
he crawled under the farmyard gate
for the last time.

Mossop! Oh Mossop. I nearly forgot. Farmer Rafferty says to be sure you go and see him before you leave just to say goodbye.
He won't shout at me again will he?

la-la-doobie-doobie-do-ho-ho - jingle-langa - dingle - dangle - d

'Of course he won't,' said Captain.
'He's happy again now. You can
hear him singing.'

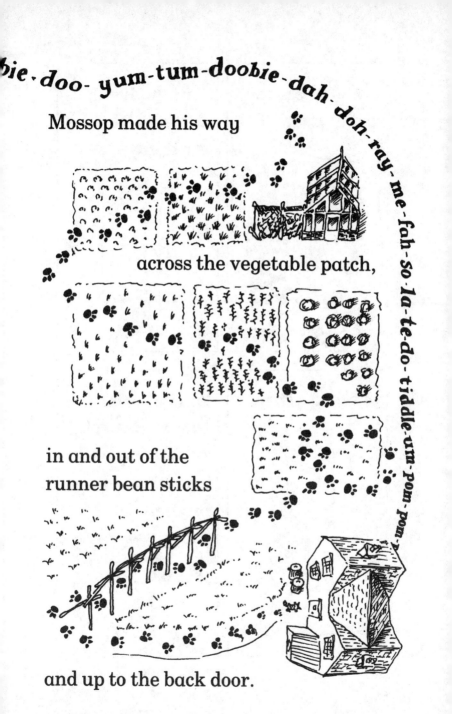

bie-doo- yum-tum-doobie-dah-doh-ray-me-fah-so-la-te-do-tiddle-um-pom-pom-

Mossop made his way

across the vegetable patch,

in and out of the
runner bean sticks

and up to the back door.

He pushed the door open...

and padded down the hallway...

to the kitchen...

Where old Farmer Rafferty was sitting with his feet warming in the oven.

AGA

'Excuse me Mr. Rafferty, but
Captain says you wanted to see me
before I went,' said Mossop. 'I haven't
got any excuses Mr Rafferty.
I tried my best but I'm just not the
cat I was. It's age, Mr Rafferty,
old age. Well, I'll be on my way now.
Goodbye Mr Rafferty.

He took Mossop to the front
doorstep, and there in front of his eyes,
were row upon row of mice and rats.

They went right up to the goldfish
pond and round and back again.

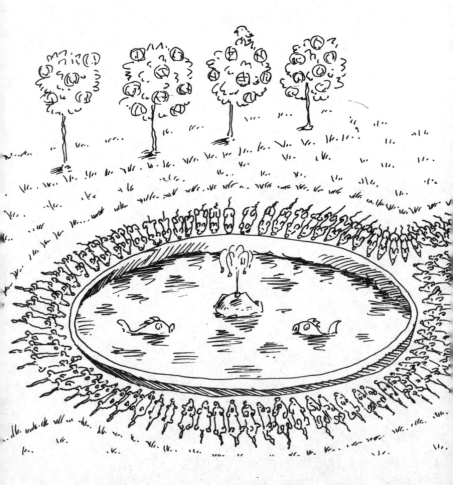

Mossop just stared and stared. He couldn't believe what he was seeing. Farmer Rafferty hung his old war medal around his neck.

My Military Medal, this is. Present from one old soldier to another, and I've no one else I'd rather give it to. You're a brave old cat and I'm proud of you. Off you go now, back to the farmyard.

Farmer Rafferty went back inside
the house shaking his head and
muttering to himself.

Then one by one they stole off into
the darkness until they were
all gone.

And he smiled as only cats can,
yawned hugely, tucked his paws
neatly under his medal, closed his
eyes and slept.

The night came down, the moon
came up, and everyone slept on
Mudpuddle Farm.

Chapter One

There was once a family of all sorts
of animals that lived in the
farmyard behind the tumble-down
barn on Mudpuddle Farm.

At first light every morning
Frederick, the flame-feathered
cockerel, lifted his eyes to the sun and
crowed and crowed until the light
came on in old Farmer Rafferty's
bedroom window.

One by one the animals crept out
into the dawn and stretched and
yawned and scratched themselves.

But no-one ever spoke a word, not until after breakfast.

Chapter Two

One morning, just after breakfast,
old Farmer Rafferty brought
Captain, the great black carthorse,
in from his field and led him into his
stable in the corner of the yard.

I'm shutting you in here, Captain. The hunt will likely be coming this way today and I don't want you galloping out after them. I'm shutting Jigger in the house as well, otherwise he'll be running off with the hounds. I'll let you both out after they've gone.

And old Farmer Rafferty went out, bolting the stable door behind him.

Captain pricked up his ears. In the
distance he could hear the hunting
horn and the baying of the foxhounds.

Soon all the animals in the
farmyard had heard it too and
were running for cover.

Peggoty rounded up her little
pigs (not forgetting Pintsize, the
littlest of them all.)

Auntie Grace and Primrose, the two dreamy-eyed cows, made off towards the barn door as fast as they could go.

While Auntie Grace and Primrose were agreeing, Egbert, the greedy goat, Diana, the silly sheep, and Frederick, the flame-feathered cockerel, ran past them into the safety of the barn.

Aunty Grace and Primrose both decided to go in at the same time.

But Albertine the white goose
stayed just where she was, sitting
serenely on her island in the pond.

Howl Yap Woof Ya

What a fuss.

Upside and Down, the two white
ducks that no one could tell apart,
were upside-down in the water so
they couldn't see or hear
what was going on.

HUBBLE
BUBBLE

GLOOP
GLOOP

It's an outright liberty!

Yap
Yap

Yap

And Mossop, who had been fast asleep on the tractor seat, shinned up the tallest lime tree and hissed with terrible fury. He hated being woken up.

Chapter Three

The hounds came through the gate.
They came over the gate and round
the gate, noses glued to the ground,
tails swishing in the air.

Behind them came red-coated, red-faced huntsmen on snorting horses that tossed their heads and flashed their eyes.

Farmer Rafferty went in to shave.
He only shaved when he remembered
to, and he remembered to now.

FADE AWAY

Chapter Four

The animals crept out of the barn
and into the bright sunlight of the
yard. They did not notice the
panting pink tongue nor the pricked
up ears of the fox as he crawled
out of a bramble hedge smiling his
sneaky smile.

Here
we go!

But Albertine did.

'Good morning, dear friends,'
he said in his sneaky voice.

And all the animals jumped in their
skins and clung to each other in fear
and trembling.

Don't be frightened, dear friends.
I ask you, do I look as
if I'd hurt a hair on your head or a
feather on your back?
It's a hard life being a fox.
Not a friend in the world. No one to
talk to. No one to play with.

He sighed a sad and sneaky sigh.
Then he cast a long and horrible
sneaky look across the pond at
Albertine.

The animals hid behind each other and kept their distance. Only Pintsize was brave enough to step forward.

I'll play with you. I can chase my own tail and catch it quick as a twick, so I can easily catch you.

But Peggoty picked little Pintsize up by his ear and dropped him under Aunty Grace's legs with all her other little pigs.

The fox wiped a sneaky tear from his eye.

Back home in my den, I have a wife and five little babies, all of them starving to death because I can't find any food to take home to them. Without food my babies will die. Won't you help me, dear friends? I beg you, think of my babies.

And all the animals thought of his babies and they could scarcely hold back their tears.

'A fox is a fox is a fox,' said Albertine
wisely from her island on the pond.
But no one was listening to her.

And they all agreed they would.

From his stable Captain could just see what was going and he whinnied his warning.

The animals thought he was calling after the huntsmen's horses – but he wasn't.

Jigger, the always sensible sheepdog,
could smell the rank smell of fox
and barked loudly from inside old
Farmer Rafferty's house.

The animals thought he was calling
after the huntsmen's hounds – but
he wasn't.

'You are so kind, dear friends,' said the fox smiling his sneaky smile. 'I don't need much. Just some milk, a few eggs, barley, wheat, oats, anything you can find. And there's no need to hurry back. Take your time.'

So one by one the animals left the yard until only Albertine was left sitting on her island.

Isn't he a jolly nice chap?

He's quite nice for a fox

What were we scared of?

And Mossop of Course...

Don't forget the old Mossop who was watching everything from his branch high up in the lime tree.

And be sure you don't forget the sneaky fox who was padding slowly towards the pond, his tail whisking to and fro, his tongue sharpening his teeth.

Chapter Five

Mossop watched in horror from his branch as the fox tested the water with his front paw,

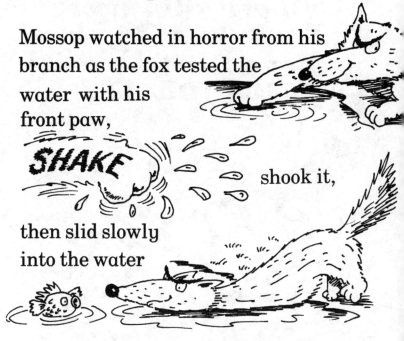

SHAKE shook it,

then slid slowly into the water

and swam out across the pond towards Albertine.

Who sat still as a statue.

Once on the island the fox shook
himself dry and licked his lips.

But Albertine sat serene and still
and looked down her nose at the fox
as he came creeping towards her.

'Mr Fox,' said Albertine, 'I am not
afraid to die. All of us have to die.
All of us have to die one day, you
know. Even you, Mr Fox. You can eat
me, but please, Mr Fox, take pity
on my children. Let them live.

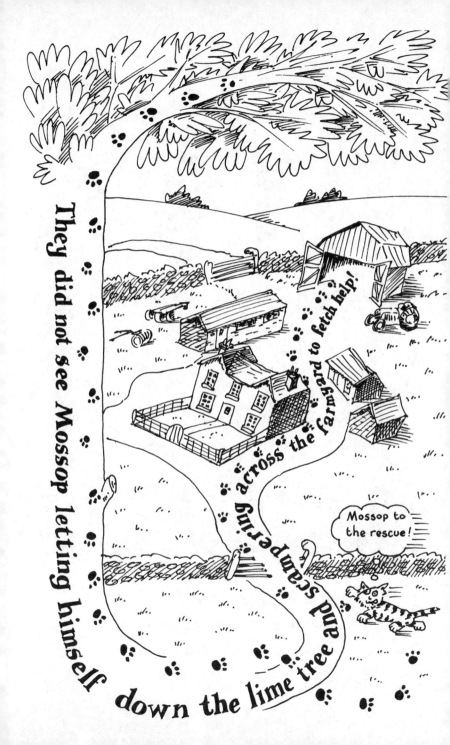

They did not see Mossop letting himself down the lime tree and scampering across the farmyard to fetch help!

Mossop to the rescue!

As Albertine spoke, she stood up
and three yellow goslings ran out
from under her feathers.

Chapter Six

The fox jumped back in surprise.

'You are brave, Madam,' he said in
a voice that was suddenly gentle
and kind, and not at all sneaky.

Five of the little perishers,
and they never stop eating.
You have three lovely children,
Madam, and they have a brave
mother. No, I just can't do it. I can't
kill you or your babies. Oh dear,
and I was so looking forward to a
nice fat goose-begging your pardon.

At that very moment the hunting
horn sounded. TARAN-TARA-

Chapter Seven

There was a terrible baying of
hounds across the fields and the
drumming of horses' hooves.
The hunt was coming back . . .

The fox looked around him on the
island, but there was nowhere to
hide. It would take too long to swim
across the pond and he knew it.
He looked at Albertine with
pleading eyes.

Won't you help me?
I beg you,
please help me.

TARAN·TARA·TARAN·

'He's got to be here somewhere,'
said the huntsman with the
ginger beard.

★ TARAN-TARA·

TARAN-TIDDLE-DOO

★ YARROOOOO

But if the red-faced, red-coated huntsmen had been in less of a hurry they would have noticed that the goose had suddenly grown

a long, red, bushy Tail!

Chapter Eight

By the time Mossop came running
back into the yard with the animals
behind him, they found Albertine
sitting quite alone on her island.

'Where is she?' asked Egbert, the
greedy goat, practising his butting.
'I'll get him, I'll get that fox.'

Even Auntie Grace (who was hardly ever angry) was lowering her head and pawing the ground like a bull.

Calm down dear!

And so, of course, Primrose did the same.

And Mossop hissed out his fury at the edge of the pond.

'I'm in here,' said the fox, as he crawled out from under Albertine's feathers, followed by three fluffy yellow goslings.

'Not me,' said the fox, shaking his head. 'Don't know what came over me. I'd better go before I change my mind.'

And he swam back across the pond and vanished over the hedge.

Chapter Nine

Later that afternoon

Upside

and Down

at last

lifted
their
heads

out of the water.

'Had a good day?' Albertine
enquired kindly, settled once again
on her goslings.

'S'pose you've been sitting there all
day doing nothing?' Upside sniggered,
or was it Down - no one could tell
the difference.

'You could say that,' Albertine said.

'Silly old goose,' said Upside, or Down, and they both turned upside-down again.

The night came down, the moon came up, and everyone slept on Mudpuddle Farm.

Pigs Might Fly!

Chapter One

There was once a family of all sorts
of animals that lived in the
farmyard behind the tumble down
barn on Mudpuddle Farm.

At first light every morning
Frederick, the flame-feathered
cockerel, lifted his eyes to the sun
and crowed and crowed
until the light came
on in old Farmer
Rafferty's
bedroom
window.

Ah sweet mystery of light, at last I've found you....

One by one the animals crept out into the dawn and stretched and yawned and scratched themselves. But no one ever spoke a word—not until after breakfast.

Old Farmer Rafferty put in his teeth, looked out of his bathroom window and shook his head.

Will it never rain again? I've forgotten what puddles look like.

All my fields are burnt yellow and the stream's dried right up.

And he opened the window and shouted,

Go away, sun! You hear me? Run off and shine somewhere else. Go on, push off!

But the sun was too far away to hear. It just went on shining.

Chapter Two

Out in the farmyard the animals
looked up at the sun and sighed.

So they all put their hats on, except
for Egbert the greedy goat who had
already eaten his –

and Pintsize
who thought pigs looked silly in
hats. But then Pintsize *never* did
what he was told.

Down at the pond Upside and
Down, the two white ducks that no
one could tell apart, had their heads
stuck in the mud because there was
hardly any water left in the pond.

Albertine sat still as a statue on her
island, shading her goslings under
her great white wings.

'When's it going to rain, Mum?'
they peeped.

'Sometime,' she said, and she
settled down to sleep because it was
the wisest thing to do and Albertine
was the wisest goose that ever lived
(and everyone knew it, including
Albertine).

So, thirsty and dusty and itchy, the animals trooped down to ask her advice, all except Mossop, the cat with the one and single eye, who was fast asleep on his tractor seat.

'What about you?' said Jigger, the almost-always sensible sheepdog.

Frederick looked up at the buzzards
and larks and swifts and swallows.
'If only I could fly like them. Must
be cool up there,' he sighed.

And little Pintsize looked up too
and thought just the same thing.

145

'You've got wings,' said Egbert.
'Use them.'

'Now, now,' said Captain. 'We're
quarrelling again.' And he called
out to Albertine.

So that's what they all did –
Captain in the darkest corner of his
stable,

Jigger under the
rhubarb leaves in
the vegetable patch,

Aunty Grace and Primrose side by
side under the great ash tree,

Egbert behind a pile of paper sacks
in the barn so he could be near his
lunch,

and Diana right in
the middle of the
sunniest field
because she was
very very silly!

Frederick went wherever his
speckled hens did – and as they all
went in different directions, he
found that very difficult!

While Peggoty and her little pigs, including Pintsize, crawled into a patch of nettles and lay still. Soon all the animals were fast asleep . . .

except Pintsize who wasn't at all sleepy.

Chapter Three

Of all Peggoty's little pigs Pintsize
was definitely the naughtiest. Say
'do this' and he'd do that. Say 'come
here', and he'd go there. It was just
the way he was. Some children are
like that.

He waited until
Peggoty was snoring,

then tiptrottered
through the
farmyard

and down the
lane

looking for really
interesting things to do.

He hadn't gone far when he saw old
Farmer Rafferty leaning on a
gatepost and talking to the
next-door farmer. Both of them
were gazing up at the sky.

Cows are lying down.
Sure sign of rain.
It's coming, I can
smell it.

Farmer Rafferty shook his head
as he squinted at the sun.

he said,
and he laughed like a drain.

Pintsize pricked up his ears, (which
isn't easy for a little pig).

And he jumped up and down
in wild excitement.

Chapter Four

Flying was not nearly as easy as it looked. Pintsize stood up on his back trotters and flapped his front ones – trotters, he thought, would do just as well as wings.

But however hard he flapped (and flapping trotters is *not* easy) and however much he jumped up and down, he somehow never managed to take off. But Pintsize was not a giving-up sort of pig. He sat down and thought about it.

The crow cackled and flew off to tell
his friends, then they all cawed
together until they got sore throats
– which served them right.

Suddenly Pintsize had an idea.

> Upside and Down,
> they can fly.
> I've seen them.
> They'll teach me.

And he trotted off down to the muddy pond. 'Upside! Down!' he squealed, but they couldn't hear him, not with their heads in the mud.

In the end he got a long stick and poked Upside in his down,

and Down somewhere else!

They were not at all pleased.

'What, like this?' they quacked.
And they took off and looped a loop.

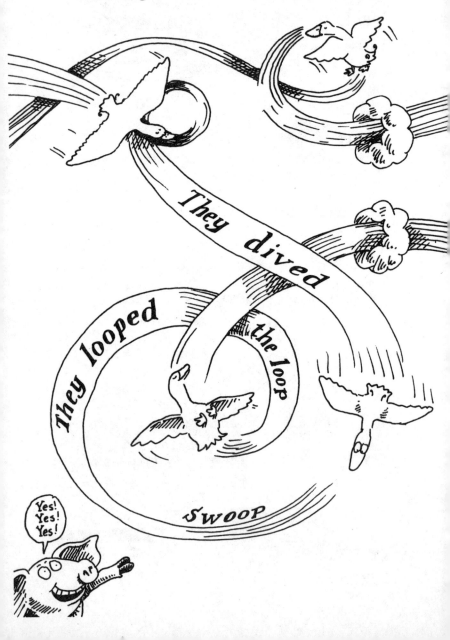

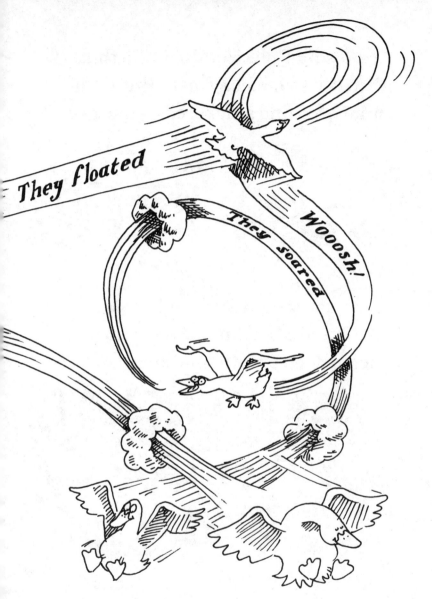

They landed quite puffed. 'Like that?' they quacked.

'Yes,' said Pintsize. 'Just like that.
Please teach me. *Please.*' But they
sniggered and snickered as ducks do.

'Just you watch me,' said Pintsize,
and he climbed up the garden wall,
took a deep breath and then ran . . .

until suddenly there was no more
wall to run on . . . and he was flying
through the air!

For one wonderful moment he was up there with the birds, but then something was pulling him down and down and down and he was turning over and over . . . .

Then he landed,

in the muddy pond.

'Oh dear,' thought Albertine. 'I suppose I'd better do something about this.'

So she stood up and honked and honked until all the animals woke up and came running.

It's Pintsize. He thinks he's a bird. look over there.

Pintsize was climbing the ladder
(and that's not easy if you're a pig)
up onto the haystack.

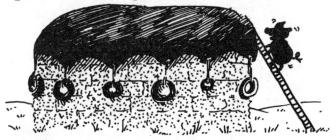

Peggoty closed her eyes, 'I'm not
looking,' she said.

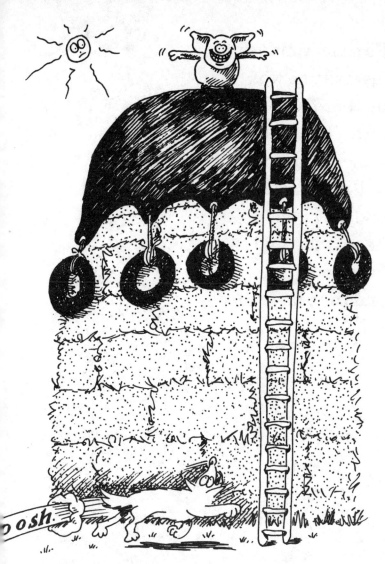

Jigger sprinted across the farmyard
until he was standing right under
the haystack. 'Don't jump!' he barked.
'Don't do it' . . . But Pintsize did it.

For one wonderful
moment he was
up there with the
birds, but then
something was
pulling him down
and down and
he was turning
over and over,
and then he landed –

SQUOOOOOF!

on Jigger's back.

Jigger never knew
that little pigs
could be that heavy.
But he knew now.

And very soon they all knew,
because wherever Pintsize went
they had to go, so that whenever he
jumped, one of them was always
there for him to land on.

Every time he jumped he flew
further – or he thought he did, 'I can
fly,' he'd squeal. 'Pigs can fly.'

And it was true – well, sort of.

Pintsize flew as far as a pig ever had
flown, but then he'd drop like a
stone and knock all the air out of
poor Aunty Grace
(and that's
a lot of air),

or Primrose

or Captain

or Egbert

or Frederick.

But the one he liked landing on
most was Diana, because she was
very soft and very springy and very
spongy.

'Thanks, Diana,' he'd squeak and off
he'd go again before anyone could
catch him.

This can't go on.
You can say that again.
This can't go on.

I've tried everything I can, he just won't listen to me.

Something's got to be done.

Too true, quite right.

But what?

Everyone looked at Albertine to see
if she'd had one of her ideas.
And of course she had.

'Don't you worry,' she said. 'I'll have a word with a friend of mine. I've got friends in high places you know. Just you keep your eye on Pintsize, all of you.'

Chapter Five

Drooping in the heat of the day, the
animals did as Albertine said and
trailed around the farm after
Pintsize. They found him teaching
his brothers and sisters. Standing
up on his back trotters, Pintsize was
explaining how a pig flies.

'You just wave these,' he said,
flapping his front trotters, 'and you
lift off. Simple when you know how.'

And all the little pigs stood up and
waved their front trotters.

I'd watch him if I
were you, Peggoty.

But I
can't
look!

While she wasn't looking, a buzzard
flew down and landed beside
Pintsize.

'Am I ready?' said Pintsize. 'Course I'm ready!' And before he knew it, the buzzard had picked him up and was soaring into the sky high above the farm.

'Nice view,' said the buzzard.

Pintsize looked down, and wished
he hadn't. His stomach started to
turn over and he began to feel very
sick and very frightened. The
animals below him were getting
smaller

and smaller.

Then he couldn't see them any
more.

'Take me down,' he squealed. 'Take me down.'

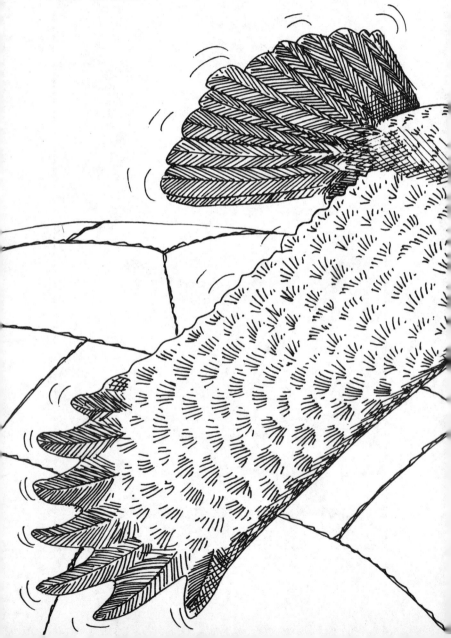

Pintsize tried to scream, but he
couldn't. He was so frightened he
couldn't even breathe . . .

The farm was coming closer and closer, it was getting bigger and bigger! He was going to crash!

Pintsize closed his eyes.

'Not yet,' said the buzzard, and as
they floated through the silent sky
they came to a cloud, a dark cloud.
'Don't like the look of that,' said the
buzzard a bit louder than he should.

Thunder rolled around the sky and
the rain began to fall in great
dollops.

'I want to go home,' squealed
Pintsize. 'I want my mama.'

'All right,' said the buzzard,
'I'll drop you off.'

And he did just that!

Down below, Farmer Rafferty was talking to the next-door farmer again.

'Yippee! Yarroo!' cried old Farmer Rafferty, and he did a sploshy rain-dance in a muddy puddle. But if he hadn't been so busy dancing, he'd have noticed that it wasn't raining cats and dogs at all – it was raining pigs. And one little pig in particular!

...int-size thumb tumbled through the air until at last he landed right in the middle of the....

DUNG HEAP

'Yes, Mama,' said Pintsize – and he
meant it. He snuggled into her and
buried his head in the dung so he
couldn't hear the thunder.

That evening Jigger saw Albertine as she was having her bath.

'Maybe,' said Albertine and smiled her goosey smile.

Peggoty put her trotters over
Pintsize's ears so he couldn't hear
any more.

'If you insist,' sulked Mossop and he
yawned hugely as cats do, closed his
one and single eye and slept.

The night came down, the moon
came up and everyone slept on
Mudpuddle farm.

Chapter One

There was once a family of all sorts
of animals that lived in the farmyard
behind the tumbledown barn
down on Mudpuddle Farm.

Cocka-doodle-doooooo

At first light every
morning, Frederick
the flame-feathered
cockerel lifted his eye
to the sun and crowed
and crowed . . .

until the light
came on in old
Farmer Rafferty's
bedroom window.

One by one the animals crept out
into the dawn and stretched and
yawned and scratched themselves;
but no one ever spoke a word, not
until after breakfast.

'Jigger my dear,' said old Farmer Rafferty, one hazy hot morning in September.

> Corn's as high as a house. Fair weather ahead, they say. Time has come for harvest, Jigger. So I shan't be needing you all day. It's your day off my dear. Old Thunder sleeps in his shed all year-now it's his turn to do some work. Got to earn his keep, just like all of us. I'll just go and rub him down.

Wooow! It's my day off!

And off he went.

'One day off a year,' thought Jigger,
the always sensible sheepdog. 'One
day a year when I don't have to be
sensible, when I can do what a dog
likes to do.' And he licked his smiling
lips, and wagged his dusty tail.

Old Thunder lived all by himself in a shed at the end of the yard. No one ever went near him because no one dared.

Pintsize had never seen Old
Thunder. He longed to peek in
through the crack in the doors.

can't quite see...

Mama,
let me look,
let me look

He squealed.

Peggoty warned him.

Don't you ever go near
Old Thunder, you hear me,
not ever.

He's a monster!
said Aunty Grace
the brown cow,

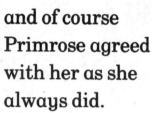

I agree.

and of course
Primrose agreed
with her as she
always did.

Matter of fact, most of the animals
thought Old Thunder was some sort
of monster.

So when old Farmer Rafferty
opened the door of the shed that
morning, all the animals went into
hiding. Upside and Down turned
upside down in terror. Mossop
disappeared into a drainpipe.
(Everyone was terrified of Old
Thunder – except Egbert the greedy
goat. He was always too hungry to
be frightened.)

DUST

I wonder if OLD
THUNDER collects
up tasty
rubbish?

Albertine the white goose gathered her goslings around her on her island in the pond and explained everything to them. She wasn't just an intelligent goose, she was a wise mother as well.

At that very and same moment, there was a roar from inside Old Thunder's shed, and he rumbled out into the yard belching smoke and dust. Old Farmer Rafferty sat high and happy on the driver's seat singing his heart out.

'See, children,' said Albertine gently. 'I told you that's all Old Thunder is, just an old combine harvester.'

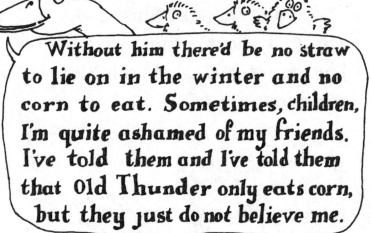

Chapter Two

Old Thunder sailed majestically out
through the gate and into the corn
field beyond, his great cutters
turning like the wheels of a giant
paddle steamer. 'One man went to
mow, went to mow a meadow,' sang
old Farmer Rafferty in his crusty,
croaky kind of voice.

to mow. went to mow a meadow.
went to mow a

And behind him, Jigger, the
usually sensible sheepdog, slunk
through the gate and lay down in
the cut corn, his nose on the
ground in between
his paws.

SNIFF

He smelt something,

and what he smelt

pleased him.

SNIFF

SNIFF

With the gate safely shut and Old
Thunder roaring round the field,
the animals at last crept out of their
hiding places and stood watching by
the gate – all except Mossop who
had fallen asleep in his drain.

ZZZZZZZZ

'What's Jigger up to?' asked Diana the silly sheep, who always asked questions but never knew any answers.

Round and round the field went old
Thunder, churning out the straw
behind him in long and golden rows.
Round and round the field went
Jigger, slinking low to the ground.

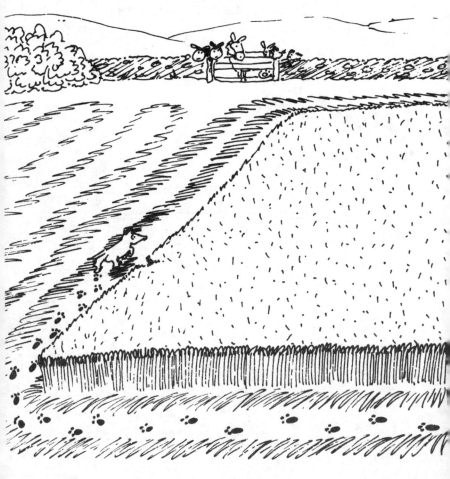

And every now and then he would
stop and stare at the square of
standing corn, and every time
he stopped, the square was a little
bit smaller.

the corn, cut the co

the way we cut

This is

'We shouldn't be standing around in the sunshine,' said Captain.

Best go inside. those flies'll be at us soon.

So they did. Except for Egbert the goat who was busy chewing off the paint from the iron-barred gate.

At eleven o'clock Old Thunder

stopped,

GRUNK!

shuddered,

RIBBLE!

coughed

SPLUT!

and was silent. The birds sang once more in the hedgerows.

Ever so carefully, for he was stiff in his knees, old Farmer Rafferty climbed down from his seat and sat down to rest in the shade.

It was time for his morning milk.
He *always* had it at eleven o'clock
no matter where, no matter what.

'I'm making sure old Thunder
doesn't miss anything,' said Jigger,
but he never took his eyes off the
standing corn.

And old Farmer Rafferty laughed
because he knew better.

Chapter Three

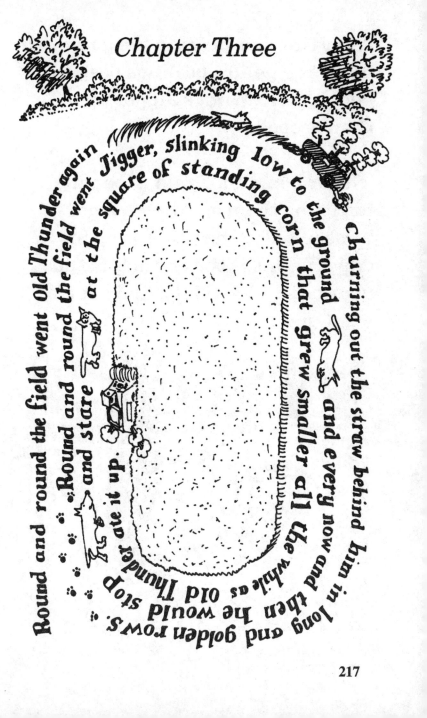

Round and round the field went Old Thunder again at the square of standing corn that grew smaller all the while as Old Thunder the field went Jigger, slinking low to the ground churning out the straw behind him in long and golden rows. Round and round the field went Old Thunder again and every now and then he would stop and stare and eat it up.

Albertine was passing the gate with her three yellow goslings peeping behind her. 'What's Jigger up to?' they peeped.

'Never you mind,' said Albertine, hurrying them on. 'Jigger's not himself today, he never is on his day off. This is the one day of the year he's not sensible, and I don't want you to watch.'

I think he's Jiggered.

'Only mad dogs go out in the mid-day sun,' grumbled Egbert the goat, who had finished eating the paint on the gate.

'Mad dogs and goats,' said Albertine, but quietly so that Egbert would not hear. She never liked to upset anyone.

I like a bit of lead free paint!

7

At one o'clock old Thunder stopped again, shuddered, coughed and was silent. The birds sang once more in the hedgerows.

Ever so carefully, old Farmer Rafferty climbed down from his seat and sat down to eat his lunch in the shade – pasties and pickles.

He offered some to Jigger for he knew Jigger was partial to pasties. But Jigger was not interested in pasties – not today – he had his eye on the golden square of standing corn.

No thanks, can't stop for lunch.

Round and round the field went
Old Thunder again

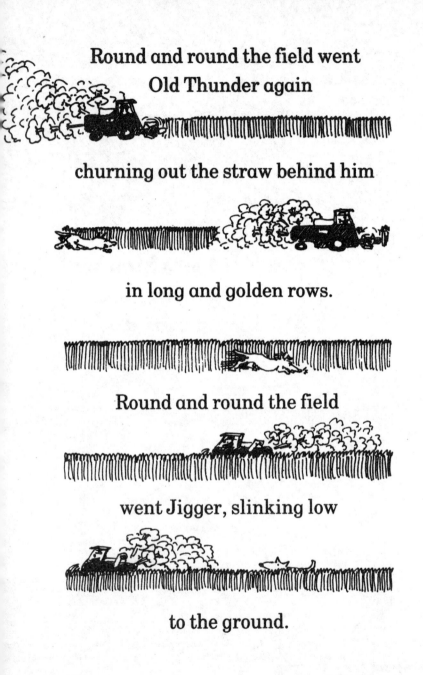

churning out the straw behind him

in long and golden rows.

Round and round the field

went Jigger, slinking low

to the ground.

Captain plodded slowly down to the pond for a drink. 'Egbert,' he said, 'is Jigger still out there in this heat?'

'Must be mad, that dog,' said Egbert. 'Hasn't stopped all day. Round and round and round he goes – makes you dizzy just to look at him. Dunno why he bothers – he never catches anything.'

At four o'clock Old Thunder stopped again, shuddered, coughed and was silent. The birds sang once more in the hedgerows. Ever so carefully old Farmer Rafferty climbed down from his seat and walked off back towards the farmhouse to fetch his tea.

'Not much more to do,' he said as he went. 'Got 'em well and truly bottled up, have you, my dear? You'll never get 'em, Jigger, you never do.'

But Jigger was not listening to old Farmer Rafferty. He lay with his chin on his paws, his ears pricked forward towards the corn, his nose twitching.

Rabbits and hares, his nose told him, rats and mice, moles and voles, pheasants and partridges, beetles and bugs.

He could hear them all rustling and bustling and squeaking and squealing in the little golden square of standing corn that was left.

Sooner or later he knew they would
have to make a run for it.

And he'd be waiting.

Chapter Four

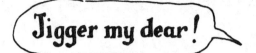

Jigger my dear!

It was old Farmer
Rafferty calling
from the house and
whistling for him.

'Jigger! Come boy, come boy! I know
it's your day off, but the sheep have
broken out in Back Meadow.
Come boy, come boy!'

I won't!
It's my one day off.
I'll be jiggered
if I'll go!

'Jigger! Jigger!' Old Farmer Rafferty
was using his nasty, raspy voice.

You come here
Jigger, else there'll
be trouble.

If I go now I'll
have wasted my
whole day. There'll
be nothing left
in that corn for
me to chase
when I get back.

And then he had an idea.

WOOF!
BARK!

Jigger's barking brought all the
animals running,

waddling

and flying
to the gate.

'Bring 'em all out into the field,
Captain,' he called out. The animals
all looked at each other nervously.

Don't worry
Old Thunder's
fast asleep.
He's been
working hard.

And so they all went out into the field, all except Diana the silly sheep who refused to go anywhere near old Thunder, whether he was asleep or not. Jigger quickly explained everything to Captain. And he went off towards the farmhouse.

In no time at all, Captain had them all organised and ready.

So Peggoty and
her little pigs,

Including Pint size!

were sent to guard the north side of
the golden square of standing corn
along with Egbert.

Primrose and Aunty Grace went off to guard the south side with Albertine and her goslings.

Captain himself stayed to guard the east side with Frederick the cockerel.

And Mossop,
the cat with
the one and
single eye
was sent off
to guard the
west side.

So on three sides of the golden
square of standing corn the animals
kept watch.

But for Mossop it was
all too much. The sun was hot

VERY HOT

SOFT AND
INVITING

and
the piles of straw so
soft and inviting.

He lay down,

closed his
one

and single
eye

and

quite forgot what he was there for.

Chapter Five

Mossop snored as he slept, and
inside the golden square of corn
they heard him and saw him
and took their chance.

One by one the little creatures of
the cornfield left their hiding
places. In one long line they left –
westwards . . .

Rabbits first, then mice and

They tiptoed past the snoring cat
and out across the open field until
they reached the safety of the
hedgerow, where they vanished.

Chapter Six

Not long after this Jigger came
haring back through the gate.

Didn't let anything
escape, did you?

Not a one.
Proper job we
did for you Jigger,
proper job.

And all the animals hurried back to
the farmyard just in case Old
Thunder woke up again – all of
them except Mossop who still lay
fast asleep in a pile of straw.

'Just this last little square to finish, Jigger,' said old Farmer Rafferty after he had finished his tea. 'Be finished by sundown, in spite of those darned sheep.'

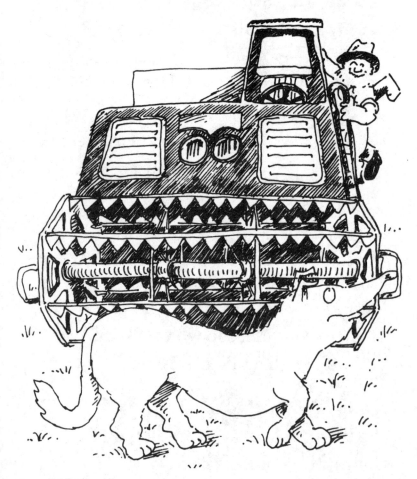

But Jigger was not listening. He
had other things on his mind. As Old
Thunder started up again he was
ready and waiting for the first of
the little creatures to break out of
their hiding place.

245

Round and round the field went Old Thunder for the last time, slinking low to the ground. Round and round the field went Jigger for the last time, and Round and Round the field

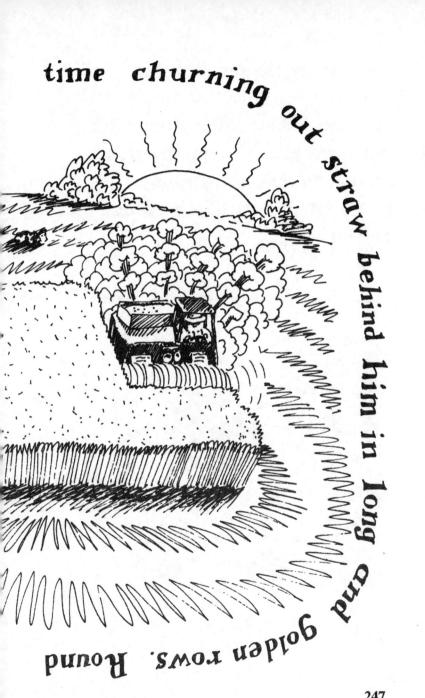

time churning out straw behind him in long and golden rows. Round

By the time the sun set behind the tumble-down barn, not a stalk of corn was left standing. And nothing had come out, no rabbit, no rat, no mouse, no vole, no mole, no pheasant, no partridge, no beetle and no bug.

Nothing.

'Well I'll be jiggered,' said Jigger.

I don't believe it!

I just don't believe it!

I could have sworn there were hundreds of them in that corn. I could smell 'em. I could hear 'em.

'It's the sun, Jigger,' said Mossop, who had just woken up. 'Does strange things to you.'

And he yawned hugely as cats do.

Jigger looked at Mossop sideways and wondered.

'Had a good day off, Jigger my dear?' old Farmer Rafferty shouted as he passed by high up on Old Thunder.

And old Farmer Rafferty laughed
and laughed, until the laughter
turned into a song once again.

w, One man and his dog, (woof! woof!) went to m
It's been a long day. Don't know about you, Jigger, but I'm just about ready for bed.
Tee hee!

And the night came down and the moon came up and everyone slept on Mudpuddle Farm.

Alien Invasion!

Chapter One

There was once a family of all
sorts of animals that lived in the
farmyard behind the tumble-down
barn on Mudpuddle Farm.

At first light every morning
Frederick, the flame-feathered
cockerel, lifted his eyes to the sun
and crowed and crowed until the
light came on in old Farmer
Rafferty's bedroom window.

One by one the animals crept out
into the dawn and stretched

and yawned

YAWNNNNNNNN

and scratched themselves.

But no one ever spoke a word – not
until after breakfast.

Early one morning old Farmer
Rafferty looked out of his window.
The corn was waving yellow in the
sun. The stream ran clear and silver
under the bridge, and the air was
humming with summer.

The bees will be out flying
today, and that means honey.
And honey means money, and I
need to buy a new tractor. The
old one won't start in the mornings,
like it should. Get busy bees.
Buzz my beauties, buzz!

Chapter Two

Deep in the beehive at the bottom
of the apple orchard, Little Bee was
getting ready for his first solo flight.

And off flew Little Bee out into the wide blue sky. Round and round he flew, looking for the clover field, but he couldn't find it anywhere.

So he buzzed down towards the old tractor where Mossop, the cat with the one and single eye, was trying hard not to wake up.

Mossop opened his eye.

Then he went back to sleep again.

The trouble was that Little Bee
didn't know his right from his left
or his left from his right.

Little Bee felt a great yawn coming
on. He looked down for somewhere
soft to sleep and then he saw the
tractor with the old cat still asleep
on the seat.

His tail looks nice
and soft and warm.
He won't mind, he
won't even know
I'm there.

And he was quite right about that.
Mossop never even felt Little Bee
land on his tail. He was too busy
dreaming. So Little Bee and Mossop
snoozed together in the sun and the
hours passed.

Chapter Three

Back in the beehive, Queen Bee
was getting worried. Little Bee had
been gone for hours now and
something had to be done.
She called all her bees together.

Right, forget pollen-gathering,
forget honey-making. Little
Bee is lost and we've got to
find him before dark else he'll
get cold and die. Follow me.

Ah-Ha!
Once more
unto the
breach!

Old Farmer Rafferty was milking
Aunty Grace, the dreamy-eyed
brown cow, when he heard the bees
coming. 'There they go,' he
chortled over his milk pail.

And then he began to sing as he
often did when he was happy.
He sang in a crusty, croaky kind of
a voice, and he made it up as he
went along.

Out in the clover field Diana the
silly sheep

was rolling on her back

to scratch her itches

when she saw a great swarm of bees
coming straight towards her.

She struggled to her feet and ran off towards the pond as fast as her legs could carry her. No one was at all surprised when she jumped right in. That's what she always did when there were bees about.

As usual it was Jigger, the almost always sensible sheep dog, who had to pull her out.

Silly sheep!

They can't sting you in the water. That's what my mother told me.

'And some mothers do have them,' thought Albertine from her island in the pond.

It's just bees buzzing. Nothing to worry about.

That's my Mum!

She's so calm in a crisis!

Best keep your head down if you ask me !

said
Upside
and Down.

So the two white ducks that no one could tell apart upside-downed themselves in the pond and stayed there all day long.

BLUB! GLUB! BLUB!

Captain, the great black carthorse who loved everyone and whom everyone loved, looked out over the clover field.

There's an awful lot of bees out there. I wonder what they're up to.

They're making honey aren't they dear?

Yes Honey!

I don't like the look of this at all. There's too many of them and....and they're coming this way!
Do pigs like honey, mummy?
I shouldn't be surprised if they do!

And sure enough, the sky above them suddenly darkened and the humming became a droning and the droning became a roaring.

But no one could move anyway.
They were all too terrified, except
Albertine of course.

'Albertine,' said Captain without
moving his lips. 'What are we
going to do?'

Chapter Four

Albertine thought her deep goosey thoughts for a moment. Then she said, 'Just follow me'. And she swam across the pond, waddled through the open gate and out into the cornfield beyond.

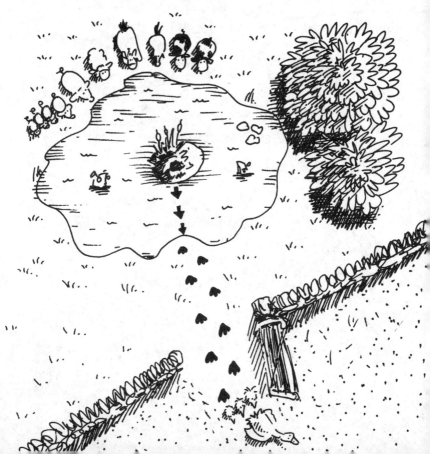

All the animals followed because they knew that Albertine was the most intelligent goose that ever lived. If anyone knew what to do, she would. They reached the middle of the cornfield and looked up. The bees were still following them.

Albertine began to run
round in a great big circle.

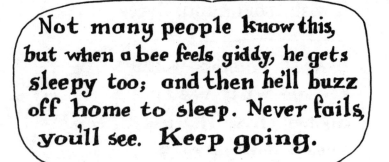

So round and round they all ran
until suddenly the buzzing stopped.
When they looked up the bees had
all buzzed off, just as Albertine had
said they would.

Chapter Five

The bees were flying home over the
farmyard when one of them
suddenly spotted Little Bee all
curled up asleep on Mossop's tail.
'Follow me,'

'I got lost,' cried Little Bee.

I want to go home.

'Soon,' Queen Bee yawned.
She could hardly keep her eyes
open, she was so sleepy.

But first
we'll hang
about here and
have a little
snooze.

And so that's what they all did.
Soon there was a great ball of
snoozing bees hanging on
Mossop's tail.

MEANWHILE....

Back in the cornfield, Captain had
a worried look on his face.
'Just look what we've done to
Farmer Rafferty's corn,' he said.
'Just look.' And they looked.

They had flattened out a huge circle in the corn. Not a single solitary stalk still stood standing.

They all heard him. He was
walking into the field singing his
honey song.

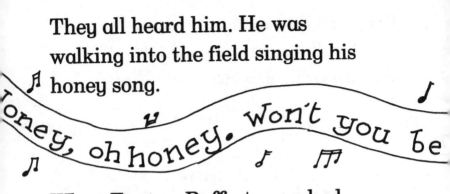

honey, oh honey. Won't you be

When Farmer Rafferty reached
the middle of the cornfield, there
wasn't an animal to be found.
What he did find was a great
circle of flattened corn.

Then off he went towards the farmhouse, counting on his fingers and muttering to himself.

He didn't know it, but from behind the farmyard wall the animals were watching and listening to every word.

'What's a Martian?' Diana asked and of course everyone looked at Albertine.

'Well,' she said, thinking very hard indeed, 'they walk stiffly like robots do and they carry ray-guns like Farmer Rafferty says.' The animals could hardly believe it, but if Albertine had told them then it had to be true. After all there was nothing Albertine didn't know.

Chapter Six

Farmer Rafferty was still counting
on his fingers when he passed by
the old tractor and noticed the ball
of bees hanging on Mossop's tail.

*Oh dear me. My bees
have gone and swarmed.
Perhaps they couldn't find
the way back home. I'll
have to put them back in
their hive.*

And he disappeared inside the
farmhouse.

While he was gone, the animals
crept back into the farmyard, just
in time to notice something coming
in through the farmyard gate.
It was dressed in white from
head to toe.

It wore a white helmet ★——

and white gloves ★——

and it walked stiffly like a robot, ★—

and as it walked it puffed smoke ★—
out of its ray-gun.

In its other hand it carried ★—
a great big sack.

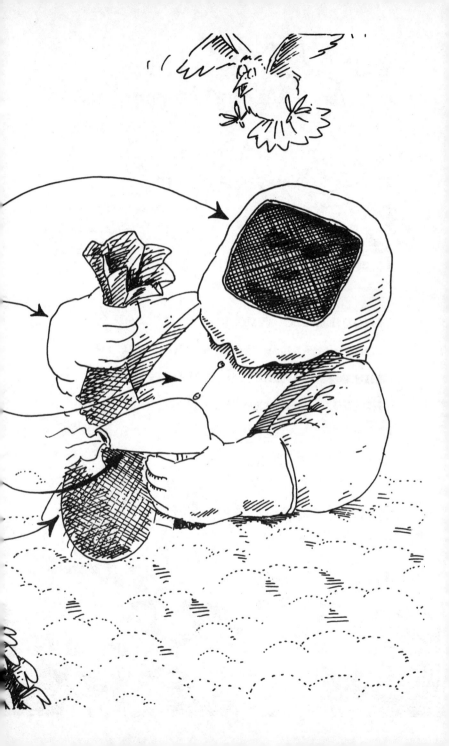

A Martian!

Diana cried. And she ran, they all ran. They ran until they came to the edge of the pond where they found Albertine washing herself.

'It's a Martian,' panted Jigger, the almost always sensible sheepdog.

Albertine smiled her goosey smile.

And they watched as old Farmer Rafferty puffed smoke around the swarm of bees.

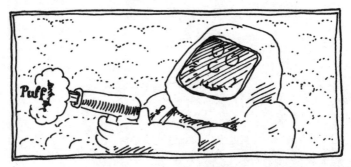

Farmer Rafferty scooped the bees
into his sack, and off he went
singing his honey song, with Queen
Bee and Little Bee and all the
others still snoozing inside.

Chapter Seven

Later that afternoon the first cars
arrived. Before long, Front Meadow
was filled hedge to hedge with cars,
and there were people everywhere.
Mossop, who had woken up by now,
walked down the lane and met
Jigger and the others.

'No one's going to believe a silly story like that, are they?' said Jigger; but when Albertine looked at him he wished he hadn't said it.

'I think,' said Albertine 'that we believe mostly what we want to believe.'

Chapter Eight

That afternoon Farmer Rafferty
showed all the visitors round his
Martian corn circle.

After that they settled down on the
front lawn to a Martian cream tea.

He told them the story of the flying
saucer and the Martians that had
landed on Mudpuddle Farm, and
they swallowed it all (the cream
teas and the story) and went
home happy.

And old Farmer Rafferty was happy
too. He'd soon have enough money
to buy his new tractor.

All red and shiny it would be, with
a proper cab on it so he could
plough his fields without getting
wet and so Mossop could sleep out
of the wind.

But Mossop was quite happy out on the old tractor in the farmyard. None of the animals ever told him about the day the bees swarmed on his tail. They thought it might give him bad dreams, and they didn't want that.

The night came down, the moon came up, and everyone slept on Mudpuddle Farm.

Chapter One

There was once a family of all sorts
of animals that lived in the
farmyard behind the tumbledown
barn on Mudpuddle Farm.

You are the sunshine of my life...

At
first
light every
morning
Frederick, the
flame-feathered
cockerel, lifted
his eyes to the sun
and crowed and crowed
until the light came on in old
Farmer Rafferty's bedroom window.

One . . . . by . . . . one,
the animals crept out into the dawn . . .

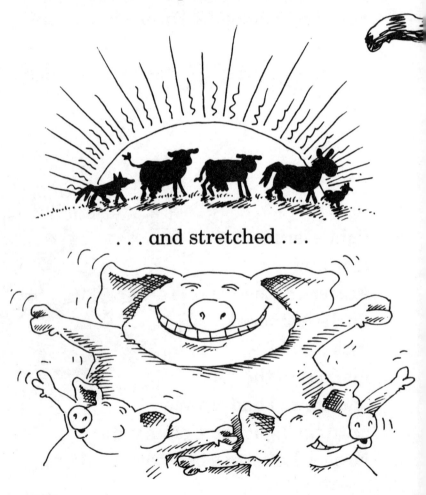

. . . and stretched . . .

. . . and yawned . . .

. . . and scratched themselves.

But no-one ever spoke a word, not until after breakfast.

One morning, Captain was crunching away at his last mouthful of breakfast hay when he noticed something was wrong.

Someone was missing. Gone!

Albertine and her little goslings were preening themselves on their island.

Upside and Down
were upside down
in the pond.

Peggoty and her little piglets,
including Pintsize, snuffled and
snorted around the dungheap.

Diana the silly sheep who couldn't
count to save her life, was counting
the clouds.

I wish I was
like a fluffy
little cloud.

You
are!

Penelope and her chicks scratched and scuffled in the orchard, never too far from Frederick.

Grace and Primrose grazed nose to nose in the meadow.

Jigger, the almost always sensible sheepdog, was chasing his tail again.

And Mossop, the cat with the one
and single eye, was
curled up asleep
on his tractor
seat as he
always
was.

BUT, where was Egbert the
grumbly goat?

Jigger,
have you seen
that grumbly
goat?

Nope,
I'll have a look
shall I?

So Jigger looked and looked.

Egbert wasn't anywhere. He'd done
a bunk, buzzed off, gone walkabout.

If anyone knows where he is, thought Jigger, Albertine will, because Albertine always knows everything. So Jigger ran down to the pond.

Albertine, have you *seen* Egbert *anywhere*? He seems to have gone *missing*.

But Egbert did not come back. The animals searched here, there and everywhere for him.

But it was no good, he couldn't
find him anywhere. No-one could
find him.

'I can't think where he's gone,' said
Grace, the dreamy-eyed brown cow.
'Nor me,' said Primrose, who
always agreed with her.

I don't know where he's gone either.

'I know, I know,'
said Diana, the
silly sheep.

He's gone missing!

'Don't worry,' Albertine told her
little goslings.

That goat will be back, you'll see, around suppertime I should think.

she's so reassuring.

Chapter Two

Sure enough, just as Old Farmer Rafferty was giving all the animals their supper that evening, Egbert wandered into the yard, grumbling as usual.

'Egbert, where have you been?' asked Farmer Rafferty in the nasty, raspy voice he kept for special occasions.

'Worried sick we were,' said Captain, the cart-horse that everyone loved and who loved everyone.

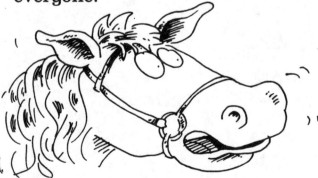

But Egbert wouldn't say another
word about it.

Down on her island in the pond, Albertine shook her head, smiled her goosey smile and thought deep goosey thoughts.

I told you he'd come back, didn't I? I'll tell you something else too, just so long as you keep mum, if you know what I mean. That goat's been up to something.

what? What? What?

Who knows? Who knows? Now, let's watch the sun go down, and then we'll all go to sleep.

Chapter Three

It wasn't long after this that Egbert
began behaving very strangely
indeed. For one thing, he stopped
grumbling. Everyone thought he
must be sick, but he wasn't.

'Good morning,' he'd say as he passed by,

...and isn't it a fine one too?

Isn't it a good day to be alive?

And he'd say that with the wind whistling through the farmyard and the rain thundering down on the corrugated roofs.

Then one day, Diana the silly sheep saw something very, very strange. She saw Egbert dancing! And he was singing too!

la la la la la

Of course none of the animals believed her at first, because Diana was always silly. But she told them and told them until they had to come and look.

And of course, when they saw it
with their own eyes they had to
believe it. Egbert was dancing in the
puddles, and singing his heart out.

in the rain.... what a wonderful feeling

...I'm happy again

SPLISH

SPLOOSH

SPLASH

SPLOSH

'He's really sick,'
said Jigger sadly.

'Hope it's not catching,' said
Penelope, hurrying her chicks away.

'He's gone loopy if you ask me,' said
Peggoty, keeping her distance at the
top of the dungheap.

Mossop opened his one and single
eye and shut it again.

I'm having a bad dream about a singing, dancing goat that's lost his marbles. I think he ought to see a vet.

But Grace and Primrose liked the song so much that they found a puddle of their own and joined in.

Albertine sighed and smiled secretly to herself.

'You'd never understand, Captain,' said Albertine; and Captain felt very stupid.

Captain couldn't understand what Albertine was talking about, but he didn't want to say so in case she might think he was as stupid as he felt he was.

Chapter Four

It was Tuesday, and Tuesday was always the day Old Farmer Rafferty went off to market.

He put on his best jacket and his best hat. Then he scooped Mossop off his tractor seat and drove to market.

Off he went, happy as a lark,
singing to himself as he always did
when he was happy though he could
never remember the words.

But Old Farmer Rafferty had
forgotten something else, too.
Something much more important
than the words. He had forgotten to
close his vegetable garden gate.

Later that morning, Egbert was
feeling even hungrier than usual.

I've chewed the last of the paint
off the gate. I've eaten the last
of the paper sacks. I've nearly eaten
my rope, but I'm still hungry.

CREAK

RUMBLE

GROAN

Then he saw Farmer Rafferty's
garden gate swinging in the wind,
squeaking on its hinges.

'Carrots,' he thought. 'Apples.'

No-one saw
him tippy-toeing
out of the farmyard
except Mossop, who
happened to open his one
and single eye as Egbert passed by.

My goat dream again, only now he's on his tippy-toes and ballet dancing!

And he went back to sleep to finish
his dream.

All morning long, Egbert chomped
and chewed his way through Old
Farmer Rafferty's carrots. No-one
noticed what he was up to until
after lunch.

Early in the afternoon, Peggoty was taking her piglets for a stroll. As usual Pintsize had run on ahead. That was why he reached the garden gate first. Pintsize knew, and all the animals knew, that none of them (except Mossop because he was special), was ever allowed inside Old Farmer Rafferty's vegetable garden.

So when he saw Egbert standing in the middle of the vegetable garden with a carrot in his mouth, he knew that there was going to be trouble, big trouble.

Pintsize loved it when other people got into trouble for a change.

Mama! Egbert is in Mr Rafferty's vegetable garden. He's eaten all the carrots!

Peggoty could not believe her eyes.
There wasn't a single carrot left
except the one in Egbert's mouth.

The little piglets gasped. Peggoty let
out her screechiest scream and
called for help.

And all the animals came running
as fast as they could.

'Egbert!' cried Captain. 'Out of there! Out of there! If Old Farmer Rafferty catches you in his vegetable garden your goose will be cooked!' And then he thought about what he'd said.

Oh, I'm sorry Albertine.

munch

munch

But Albertine just smiled.

See? I told you Captain, didn't I? Carrots.

But Captain still didn't understand.

'I'll get him out,' said Jigger, the almost always sensible sheepdog. He dashed into the garden and tried to pull Egbert out by his rope. But Egbert would not budge.

Captain came in to help as well but still Egbert dug his heels in and would not move.

Oh come on Egbert. Old farmer Rafferty will be back in a minute.

In fact, Old Farmer Rafferty was just at the end of the farm lane, talking to Farmer Farley from the next door farm. 'Goats,' Farmer Farley was saying, 'who'd have them? They go where they want, eat what they want, do as they please. Still they make you laugh don't they?' And the two of them just laughed and laughed.

Back in the farmyard, the animals all heard Farmer Rafferty coming up the lane on his tractor. He was still singing away.

'I'm off,' said Jigger.

'Me too,' said Captain.

But Albertine decided to wait.
'I think I'll just stay and see what
happens,' she said.

Pintsize hid under Albertine's wings
and pretended to be a gosling.

As Old Farmer Rafferty came
through the garden gate, all the
animals hid behind the wall and
watched.

Suddenly, Old Farmer Rafferty
stopped singing. With bated breath,
the animals waited for him to shout
in his nasty, raspy voice. But he
didn't.

All he said was:

You silly old goat, eating all my lovely carrots. Still, I expect you need them more than I do.

And Farmer Rafferty laughed and laughed. He picked up Egbert's rope and led him out into the orchard.

You have all the apples you can find my dear. You'll get fat, but that doesn't matter does it? You eat as much as you like.

The animals could not believe their
ears. They could not understand
it at all. But Albertine could. She
smiled her goosey smile and
waddled off back to her pond. Then
she climbed up on to her island and
tucked her head under her wing
and slept. There were four little
goslings under her wing that night,
and one of them had trotters.

Chapter Five

It turned out just as Old Farmer
Rafferty had said. Egbert did get
fat, very fat. It wasn't surprising –
he did nothing but eat all day long.

He ate anything and everything –

Captain's
best hay,

Jigger's
biscuits,

Peggoty's
pigmeal,

Penelope's
corn,

Diana's
sheepnuts,

and Old Farmer Rafferty's socks off
the washing line.

He even ate the sack that Mossop
used for his bed on the tractor seat.
'I'm not dreaming this,' said
Mossop, yawning hugely. 'That goat
is eating my bed.' Mossop was not
at all happy about that.

No-one knew what to do, but they all knew something had to be done. So they went off to ask Albertine. If anyone knew what to do she would.

But Albertine was being very secretive. 'Mum's the word,' she said inscrutably, and she would say no more.

'Well I think that goat needs to lose some weight,' said Grace, the dreamy-eyed brown cow.

'Jogging,' said Jigger.

So five times a day all the animals, except Albertine who would sing along quite happily, and danced in any puddles he could find. Afterwards they did their aerobics, and all the while Egbert thought it was all very silly, jogged round Front Meadow.

Ridiculous!

'I'm singing in the sun, singing in the sun,' (or rain, depending on the weather). He didn't seem to mind the exercise at all, just so long as he could carry on eating afterwards.

And that's just what he did. He got fatter,

and fatter,

and fatter.

And to everyone's amazement, he stopped grumbling completely. The animals could not believe it.

'I'm just the happiest, luckiest goat
in the whole wide world,' he said
jumping into another puddle.

'What's he got to be so happy
about?' said Jigger. 'What's
happened to him?' And he went to
ask Albertine again.

But Albertine was keeping mum.
'Mum's the word,' she said
inscrutably, and she smiled a secret
goosey smile again.

Chapter Six

Then one morning, Captain was looking out of his stable after his breakfast, when he saw that Egbert had vanished again.

No-one could find him anywhere. All day long they looked but they still couldn't find him.

At last they went to tell Old Farmer
Rafferty the bad news.

We've lost him again, we've lost Egbert!

But instead of saddling Captain and
going out to look for him, Old
Farmer Rafferty just leant on his
spade and laughed and laughed.

Why don't
you have a
look through
my sitting-
room window?

Jigger got there first.

'Oh yes he can,' laughed Old
Farmer Rafferty. 'He can and he
has because *he* is a *she*.
Egbert is Egberta,
and she's just had
two lovely kids.'

And they all
peered in at the
window. There was
Egberta lying out on
the sofa, a cushion under her head,
with her two little kids beside her.

That evening, Farmer Farley
brought Billy, his billygoat over to
Farmer Rafferty's to see his kids.

'It's my Egberta who's the clever one, bless her,' said Farmer Rafferty.

'I'd say they're both clever,' said Farmer Farley.

Meanwhile, Billy chewed the paint off the window and Egberta chewed the sofa, and both of them looked very happy indeed.

Chapter Seven

Out on the pond, Upside and Down
came up for a breather. 'Anything
new happened?' they asked.

'Not me,' Albertine smiled.
'Egberta. She's the one that's
kidding. It'll be nice to have some
real kids around won't it
children?'

She cuddled her goslings under her wings, including the one with the trotters. 'Do you want a story to send you to sleep?' And of course they did.

The night came down, the moon came up and everyone slept on Mudpuddle Farm.